Winnie *Dancing* on Her Own

Winnie *Dancing* on Her Own

by Jennifer Richard Jacobson
Illustrated by Alissa Imre Geis

Houghton Mifflin Company

The author wishes to acknowledge
Ann Rider for her wonderful insights and ear.

Text copyright © 2001 by Jennifer Richard Jacobson
Illustrations copyright © 2001 by Alissa Imre Geis

www.houghtonmifflinbooks.com

The text of this book is set in Utopia.
The illustrations are pencil.

Library of Congress Cataloging-in-Publication Data

Jacobson, Jennifer, 1958–
Winnie (dancing) on her own / written by Jennifer Richard Jacobson;
illustrated by Alissa Imre Geis.
p. cm.
Summary: Winnie is worried when her best friends Zoe and Vanessa
enroll her in ballet classes with them, since she would rather go to the library
and read as they always have.
RNF ISBN 0-618-13287-2   PAP ISBN 0-618-36921-X
[1. Friendship — Fiction. 2. Ballet — Fiction. 3. Individuality — Fiction.]
I. Geis, Alissa Imre, ill. II. Title.
PZ7.J1529 Wi 2001
[Fic] — dc21   00-053929

Manufactured in the United States of America
QUM 10 9 8 7 6 5

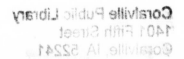

For my father, my first dancing partner
—*J. R. J.*

For Corrie
—*A. I. G.*

Chapter 1

"Do you want jam or bananas on your peanut butter, Dad?"

"What did you say, Winnie?" asked Mr. Fletcher.

Winifred, or Winnie as her friends and her dad called her, pulled down the newspaper page in front of her father's nose. "Jam or bananas on your peanut butter?

"Mmmm." he thought for a moment.

"Bananas have potassium, Dad. The jam has a tiny bit of vitamin C." It was Winnie's job to make a healthy lunch for herself and her father. She took her job very seriously.

"Bananas then," said Mr. Fletcher.

Winnie cut the sandwiches in little triangles, wrapped them in wax paper, and put them in their cloth lunch bags. Winnie's bag had a picture of the Earth and the words *Care for Me* on it. Mr. Fletcher's bag had a picture of a kite on it.

"Don't forget to call Mrs. Wiley and Mrs. Johnson about Friday night."

"Friday night? What's Friday night?"

"Dad!"

"Wait, wait." Mr. Fletcher grabbed sheets of paper from the center of the table and rolled them into a wizard's hat. He held the hat on his head with one hand and put his other hand across his forehead. "I see three girls giggling in sleeping bags. Of course!" he shouted. "You want to have Vanessa and

Zoe sleep over on Friday. I'll call their mothers today."

"Do you want me to write you a note to remind you, Dad?"

"That's okay, Win. You'd better run."

"See you later, Gator." Winnie gave her father a kiss on the cheek and went out on the porch to wait for Vanessa.

Most of the houses in Winnie's neighborhood were built for two or three families. Vanessa Wiley lived on the second and third floors of Winnie's house. Her bedroom floor was Winnie's bedroom ceiling. Vanessa had moved there three years ago, when they were five. She had long curly hair and a voice that sounded like singing. She wanted to be an actress when she grew up.

"*Black socks, they never get dirty,*" Vanessa sang as she bounced down the stairs.

Winnie joined in.

"*The longer you wear them, the stiffer they get.*
Sometimes I think of the laundry, but something keeps telling me, don't send them yet."

"Show your socks! Show your socks!" cried Winnie.

Vanessa lifted up the leg of her jeans to show Winnie her black socks.

Just as Winnie was showing her black socks to Vanessa, Zoe Johnson came up the front steps. Zoe and Winnie had been friends since they were babies. Zoe wasn't like Vanessa. She was quiet and shy. She knew all her multiplication tables when she was in second grade. Winnie thought she was probably the smartest kid in the whole third grade.

"Show your socks, Zoe," said Winnie.

Zoe lifted her pant leg and smiled. Black socks, of course.

When Vanessa moved into Winnie's

house, Zoe was sad. "Now you and Vanessa will be best friends," she had said.

"The three of us can be best friends," said Winnie. And that's what they were, three best friends.

Chapter 2

"Girls, you're going to be late!" shouted Mrs. Wiley, Vanessa's mother, from an upstairs window. "Get walking!"

Winnie hooked one arm in Vanessa's and one arm in Zoe's and they zigzagged up the sidewalk chanting:

"My back aches,
My boot's too tight,
My feet bake,
To the left, to the right."

Zoe's older brother had taught them that

chant. The girls were always looking for sayings that no one else at school would know. To Winnie, they were like passwords for a secret club.

When they reached the end of Clementine Street, the girls turned left, walked two blocks, and waited for the crossing guard to wave them across the street to school.

"Here they are now," said Mrs. Russell, the crossing guard. "The tremendously terrific trio!"

Winnie loved it when people talked about them that way. Mrs. Russell walked them across the street and said, "Okay, let me guess. What's the same today?"

She looked at their hair, their shirts, their shoes. "I give up," she said. The girls lifted their pant legs.

"Black socks! Bless me!" Mrs. Russell shook her head and hurried back to help a first-grader cross the street.

The playground was crowded. Winnie knew from the number of kids that they were later than usual today. Now they would have only a few minutes to talk before school started.

"Quick! Let's plan our sleepover," said Winnie.

Zoe opened her binder to record their ideas in her notebook.

Winnie glanced at the neat pages of Zoe's notebook. Her cursive writing was slanted perfectly and stayed within the lines. There were no eraser marks. Winnie saw the word *Homework* written at the top of one page.

"Oh, no!" she yelled.

"What?" asked Vanessa.

"I left my homework at home!"

"Didn't you leave it on the table like you always do?" asked Vanessa.

"Yes, but—" Winnie tried to think back. Why hadn't she picked up her homework?

"I was reminding my father about the sleepover . . . and Dad rolled my writing into a wizard's hat!"

Zoe and Vanessa looked at each other. Winnie caught the look. She knew what her friends were thinking. They were thinking that her father wasn't like other fathers. That he was sillier, more like a kid.

"Are you sure you don't have it?" asked Zoe.

"Yeah," said Winnie. "Now I won't be able to come out for recess." That was the third-grade rule. If you didn't have your home-work, you had to stay in and do it again.

Winnie felt her throat tighten. She had worked hard on this homework assignment.

Now her teacher, Mr. Barth, would prob-ably think she hadn't done the assignment. But even worse, she wouldn't be able to see Zoe and Vanessa until the end of the day. They were in different classes this year and had only one recess a day together. She hated it when things didn't go as planned.

"We can wait and plan the party after school," said Zoe. "It won't be fun without you."

"We could throw away our homework," said Vanessa. "Then we would all have to stay in for recess."

Winnie instantly felt better. She couldn't

believe her friends would do that for her. But then she remembered that Vanessa had mean Mrs. Twitchy. She would probably yell at her for not having her work. And Zoe had probably never stayed in for recess before. It would ruin her record.

"No," said Winnie. "Even if you stayed in, we wouldn't be able to talk to each other.

We can plan at the library this afternoon."

Vanessa and Zoe just nodded.

"Thanks anyway," said Winnie.

The bell rang and Winnie lined up with her class. She gave a little wave to Vanessa and Zoe in their lines, and then she went into school to face this day alone.

Chapter 3

The first thing Mr. Barth did every morning was ask the class to take out their homework. Then the homework monitor would walk around and check off people's names on a list. If you did your homework, the monitor put a plus sign next to your name. If you didn't have it, the monitor put a take-away sign. A minus. That's what Winifred Fletcher would get today. A big fat *minus*.

To make matters worse, Cynthia was the homework monitor. She wouldn't quietly put a minus next to Winnie's name and move on to the next person. She would say something loud like, "Don't you have your homework, Winnie?" Everyone would turn and look.

"How come you don't have your homework?" Cynthia asked loudly.

"I left it at home," Winnie replied in a voice barely above a whisper. Everyone turned to look at her.

"You know, you should have a system," said Cynthia. "You should always put your homework in the same place."

Winnie wanted to say, *I* do *have a system. It just didn't work.* But she didn't say anything. Cynthia moved on to the next person.

"After announcements, some of you may want to read what you wrote last night to the class," said Mr. Barth.

Her class had to write about their pets. Winnie didn't have a pet. Her father said that the two of them already had too many things to think about. So Winnie had written about an imaginary cat named Mr. Edgar.

Winnie would have loved to have read her story about Mr. Edgar out loud. *I know,* she thought. *I'll read it to Zoe and Vanessa at the sleepover on Friday. They'll love it.*

"I have two announcements," said Mr. Barth. "First, we need to do a better job of cleaning up our room at the end of the day. The custodian finds too many pencils and scraps of paper on the floor at night."

"Second," Mr. Barth picked up a short piece of paper and read, "A ballet class will be offered after school on Tuesday afternoons. All interested students should go to the gym during recess to learn more about the class."

Winnie was not an interested student. Ballet sounded too much like the movement and music class she had taken in first grade. When the other kids were being gentle breezes, the teacher said Winnie was a tornado. When the other children danced like swans, Winnie danced like a goose with something stuck in her throat. She could not touch her head with her toes. She could not lie on her belly and hold her ankles and rock. She simply could not dance without falling over her feet. Besides, on Tuesdays Winnie and her two best friends always went to the public library.

They spent every afternoon together. Mondays, Wednesdays, and Fridays they went to an after-school program at the YMCA. Thursdays was Girl Scouts. On Tuesdays they went to the library. Tuesday was Winnie's favorite day.

"Who would like to read his or her pet piece first?" asked Mr. Barth.

Sherry did. She read a story about how her dog protected their apartment from a burglar. Winnie wished that she had thought to have Mr. Edgar save somebody.

When Cynthia read about her goldfish, Winnie's mind wandered. She wondered what Vanessa and Zoe were doing right now. She wondered what they would do at recess. Winnie usually came up with the recess plan. She wondered what they would choose to play without her.

Chapter 4

At recess, Winnie joined the line of kids who had to walk down to Mrs. Twitchy's room. Mrs. Twitchy was the homework teacher for the day.

"You didn't do your homework, Winifred?" asked Mr. Barth as he led the group down the hall. He always used proper names when he was being stern.

Winnie wanted to defend herself. She wanted to say, *I did do my homework, but my father used it as a hat,* but she knew it would sound ridiculous. And besides, Mr.

Barth had a "no excuses" homework rule.

Winnie sat down in the front row of the classroom to rewrite her story. Vanessa had told her that Mrs. Twitchy was kinder to the kids who sat near the front.

She took out a sheet of notebook paper and began writing. The sun poured into the room, making Winnie sweat. She wished she could ask Mrs. Twitchy if she could open the windows for air. But Mrs. Twitchy was still wearing a sweater buttoned over her polkadot dress.

Joey leaned over and whispered something to the boy next to him. Everyone looked up. Mrs. Twitchy stared at Joey for at least four minutes. She didn't say a word. She just stared.

From then on, the room was totally quiet except for the sound of pencils moving on paper or the sound of a chair scraping the floor when someone had to change the way she was sitting. In fact, the whole school was quiet. With the windows closed, Winnie couldn't even hear the sounds of the other kids playing outside.

Winnie finished her story and wondered what she should do now. She decided to go back and add a part about Mr. Edgar saving a girl from drowning in the Charles River.

After that, she still had time left over, so she tore out another sheet of notebook paper and began writing a list of things she and Vanessa and Zoe could do at their sleepover party.

1. Turn off the lights in the apartment and play Sardines.
2. Play the "What would you do if" game.
3. Make fudge and eat the whole batch.
4. Tell what animals people remind you of.
5. Fall asleep watching "The Parent Trap" (the old one) for the hundredth time.

Winnie was so involved in writing her list that she didn't see Mrs. Twitchy standing over her.

"I'll take that," said Mrs. Twitchy.

Winnie handed the list to her. Mrs. Twitchy moved her eyeglasses up on her nose and read. Just then, the bell marking the end of recess rang. Mrs. Twitchy squished the list into a ball and told the kids to go back to their classes.

"Winnie!" Zoe yelled. The girls always waited for one another at the fire hydrant after school. And they always called the same thing as one or another came out through the heavy school doors: "We're over here!"

"Vanessa, how do you put up with Mrs. Twitchy all day?" Winnie asked. "She's so mean!"

Vanessa made her face look just like Mrs. Twitchy's did when she was staring at Joey. "Did she give you the Twitchy stare?"

Winnie started to tell the girls about how Mrs. Twitchy had taken the sleepover party list, but Zoe quietly interrupted. She had her own news.

"These are for you." Zoe handed papers to Winnie and the three girls started walking toward the library.

"Isn't it great, Win?" asked Vanessa.

"What are they?" asked Winnie. There was a schedule on one sheet of paper and a list of things to wear on another.

"There's going to be a ballet class on Tuesdays. Zoe and I heard about it during recess," Vanessa said.

"But don't worry, Winnie," said Zoe. "We signed you up, too."

"We start next week," said Vanessa. "You have to get your dad's permission."

"And you have to buy some of the things on this list," said Zoe.

It never occurred to Winnie that Vanessa and Zoe would want to take ballet. She hadn't heard either of them mention dance before.

"We can't sign up for ballet," said Winnie, stopping cold. "We go to the library on Tuesdays."

"We could skip the library for a while," said Zoe.

"I'm sick of the library anyway," said Vanessa. "Keep walking, Winnie."

Vanessa started to tell Winnie all about the routines they would learn and about a recital that they would give at the end of the session. Winnie couldn't believe her ears. Going to the library was her favorite thing to do. She thought Vanessa and Zoe felt the same way.

"Well, you two can take ballet," said Winnie. "I'm going to keep coming here."

The girls had arrived at the library, and passed through stone arches to reach the front door. Vanessa and Zoe looked at Winnie with surprise. They almost never disagreed.

"We don't have to decide now," said Zoe. "Let's go pick out some books."

Winnie didn't say anything. It felt like her friends were ganging up on her. They didn't care whether she wanted to dance or not. Somehow, she mattered less to them now than she had earlier that morning when they had offered to stay in for recess.

She turned and entered the cool, dark library. Vanessa and Zoe followed.

They returned their books in the book

drop and headed for the stacks. Winnie immediately went to the mystery section. She had decided to read every book in a series. She picked up number 6, one of her favorites, and read: "The campfire burned low. Frankie finished her cocoa and looked up at the stars in the sky. That's when she heard the twig snap behind her. She turned quickly. Someone was there! Someone was watching her."

Frankie is so brave, thought Winnie as she put the beloved book back on the shelf. There were forty-three books in this series, Winnie had just finished number 24. She could read two in a week, so she looked for numbers 25 and 26. Fish guts! Number 26 was out. Winnie would have to skip it and read 27. She hated when she had to skip.

"Are you ready, Win?" asked Zoe. Winnie shrugged and followed Zoe to the back stairway of the library. The librarians didn't want children going to the adult section. But Winnie, Zoe, and Vanessa moved so quietly, they were seldom seen. They went all the way back to the section where authors' names began with U, V, W, X, Y, and Z. The girls loved that their own first names began with these end-of-the-alphabet letters.

The three girls scrunched up in the corner of the stacks to read. They arranged their jackets and their backpacks to make comfortable resting spots. Winnie opened her book and tried reading *The Mystery of the Lost Treasure,* but she found herself reading the same line over and over. How could Zoe and Vanessa sign her up for ballet without asking her?

"What are you reading?" Winnie heard Vanessa whisper. She looked up and saw that Vanessa was whispering to Zoe.

"*The Youngest Ballerina,*" whispered Zoe. "That looks good," said Vanessa. "Can I read with you?" Vanessa slid over and looked at the ballet book with Zoe.

Chapter 5

"Did you get the chocolate, Dad?"

"Sorry, Win, but Vinnie's was out of unsweetened chocolate," Mr. Fletcher said as he pulled carrots and yogurt out of the grocery bags.

"How are we going to make fudge tonight?" asked Winnie. The girls were to arrive any minute and Winnie wanted everything to be perfect. No—better than perfect.

"Let's see," said Mr. Fletcher as he opened and shut cupboards. "There's got to be something that will work in here if we

use the Fletcher imagination. Tuna Helper?
Canned beets? How about some sardines?"

Winnie groaned.

"Here are some graham crackers," said
Mr. Fletcher.

"They've gone soft," said Winnie.

"And some marshmallows . . . "

"They're hard as rocks," said Winnie. But suddenly she understood. "You bought chocolate bars!"

Sure enough, Mr. Fletcher pulled chocolate bars out of the bag. They could make s'mores. The microwave would melt the chocolate, marshmallows, and crackers into a gooey, delicious snack.

The doorbell rang. Both girls arrived at the same time. They each carried a sleeping bag, a pillow, and a backpack. Vanessa was also carrying her stuffed monkey, Bobo.

The girls spread their sleeping bags out on Winnie's floor. They unpacked their backpacks. Vanessa took out her pajamas and put them under her pillow. Zoe took out the ballet book from the library. Winnie tried not to let it bother her. She had so many fun things planned for them, there would be no time for reading.

"What do you want to do first?" asked Winnie.

Vanessa and Zoe both shrugged.

"I'll tell you what was on the list I wrote," said Winnie. She told them her ideas, but instead of saying, "making fudge," she said "making s'mores."

"What do you want to do first, Winnie?" asked Zoe.

"Let's eat s'mores," said Winnie. She couldn't get her mind off them.

"Okay," said Vanessa.

"I don't think I'll have a s'more," said Zoe.

"Why not?" both Winnie and Vanessa

asked at the same time. They knew Zoe loved chocolate.

"Ballet dancers need to have strong, healthy bodies. I'm going to try to eat healthy foods from now on."

Winnie ate healthy foods. She always made healthy lunches for herself and her dad. But no more s'mores? This ballet thing was definitely going too far.

"I guess you're right," said Vanessa. "We probably shouldn't eat junk food."

Winnie felt herself turning purple. How come her friends didn't remember how badly she danced? How come they didn't remember that the teacher always put Winnie at the end of the bunny-hop line so she wouldn't confuse the other children? How come they didn't care?

"Let's play the 'What would you do if' game!" shouted Vanessa. Vanessa loved this game.

"You can go first, Winnie," said Zoe.

"Okay," said Winnie. What else could she do? She didn't want to have an argument tonight. The three friends lay on their backs. It was easier to be truthful this way.

"What would you do if you were in Vinnie's Convenience Store and you saw someone shoplift something?" asked Winnie.

"I'd tell Vinnie so he could stop it," said Zoe.

"What would you do, Vanessa?" asked Winnie.

"I'd tell the person who stole something that I saw her."

"Or him," said Winnie.

"You would?" asked Zoe. "What if the person had a gun or something?"

Vanessa thought for a moment. "Maybe the person really needed food."

"That doesn't make stealing okay," said Zoe.

"I've heard some kids brag about stealing from Vinnie's," said Winnie.

"That makes me mad!" said Vanessa. "Vinnie's so nice." But then her face turned cheerful again. "My turn!" she said. "What would you do if your dance teacher asked you to try out for the Boston Ballet?"

Winnie sighed. Last week her friends never mentioned ballet. Now it was all they could think of.

"That would be so scary," said Zoe. "I don't think I could do it."

"It would be hard," said Vanessa. "I would love it if I got a part in *The Nutcracker*, but I'd be so disappointed if I had to play a rat or—something."

"I'd sell all my toe shoes," interrupted Winnie, "and buy myself a plane ticket. Then I'd fly to the desert and find the bones of a dinosaur that had never been discovered. People from all over the world would come to see my dinosaur. I would never think of dancing again."

Winnie stopped talking. There was a long silence. Finally Zoe spoke up.

"*Please, Winnie.* We don't want to take ballet lessons without you."

"Remember when we took that music and movement class in first grade? That was fun," said Vanessa.

"Fun for *you*," said Winnie.

"Please try it, Winnie. You haven't tried to dance since you were six." said Zoe. "If you don't like it, we'll all quit."

"Please say yes, Win," Vanessa pleaded.

"If I say yes, will you promise not to mention ballet for the rest of the sleepover?"

Vanessa and Zoe chanted together,

"Cross my heart.
Hope to die.
Stick a needle in my eye."

"Okay," said Winnie. Ballet was not mentioned again that night. But that didn't mean that Winnie didn't think of it. *What did I get myself into?* she wondered as they watched *The Parent Trap* for the hundredth time.

Chapter 6

Winnie opened the bag her father had given her. Inside was a pair of pink tights and a pink leotard. She held the tights up. They were as long as the distance from her nose to her toes. She looked at the tag: size 14. Winnie took a size 10.

"I know you take a smaller size, Win. But when I held the tights up, they looked so tiny. Nothing like my stringbean Winnie."

"Tights always look small, Dad. They stretch when you put them on."

"I'm sorry, Winnie. I guess I'm just not very helpful when it comes to this stuff. Your mother would have known what tights to buy you."

Winnie had never known her mom. She had died soon after Winnie was born. Sometimes Winnie missed having a mom. But she didn't miss her mom the way her dad did. He'd had time to love her.

"I don't think I'll be much of dancer," Winnie whispered.

"Because of the outfit?" asked Mr. Fletcher.

"No, it's not that. I just don't think I'll do very well."

"Winnie, you can do anything you want

to do. Have confidence in yourself. If you want me to exchange the tights . . ."

Winnie held up the leotard and tights. "These will be fine, Dad. I can make them work." Winnie didn't tell her dad that all the other girls would choose black, not pink, leotards with silky black skirts.

Just then they heard loud footsteps as Vanessa bounded down the stairs—two at a time—in the front hallway. The doorbell rang and Vanessa let herself in before either Mr. Fletcher or Winnie could say a word.

"Hi, Mr. Fletcher. My mom said there was a sale on dance outfits at Daley's today. She bought an extra pair of tights and a leotard and a dance skirt in case Winnie could use them for lessons tomorrow."

Mr. Fletcher smiled. "What would we do

without your mother, Vanessa?" he said.

"She said not to worry if you already have some. My sister, Marisa, can always wear them in a year or two."

"As a matter of fact, we do need tights," said Mr. Fletcher.

"Thanks, Vanessa," said Winnie. "I could use the tights and the skirt. But tell your mother that my father bought me a leotard that I can wear."

Vanessa looked at the pink leotard. "Are you sure?"

"I'm sure," said Winnie.

"Okay. But let's wear our lockets so you, me, and Zoe will be the same."

Later Winnie tried on the pink tights, the pink leotard (it was just one size too big), and the black silky skirt. She could hear her father talking to her grandmother on the phone in the next room.

"Winnie's taking ballet," he said. "Of course. She'll love it, Mom. She's very excited." Winnie searched her drawers until she found her locket. Inside was a picture of her mother.

"Did you ever take ballet, Mom?" Winnie asked. "I bet if you did, you looked like a swan and not a droopy goose like me."

Chapter 7

During the first lesson, their ballet teacher, Mrs. Blair, taught them the five positions and how to stretch and strengthen their muscles at the *barre*. She knew that the girls and the three boys who took the class were beginners, and she was patient when they didn't stand straight or keep their balance.

During the second lesson, Mrs. Blair made everyone stop and look at perfect Cynthia.

"See how straight her back is," said Mrs. Blair. "See how gracefully she holds her arms in the air. See how her fingers extend to make her whole body a perfect line."

Cynthia's face didn't even change expression while Mrs. Blair was talking. Winnie did not really care that she couldn't dance like Cynthia. And she was used to Cynthia being perfect. But she felt bad for Vanessa and Zoe. Winnie could tell that they wished Mrs. Blair had stopped the class to point out how well they were doing.

On the third Tuesday, the class got worse. Suddenly, Mrs. Blair wasn't as patient. She expected everyone to remember

the five positions. She expected everyone to know the name of the barre exercises. She wanted everyone's body to be one straight line.

"In two weeks," said Mrs. Blair, "parents will be invited to see the progress we've been making. I want to show them some progress!"

"*Plié!*" called Mrs. Blair.

Winnie looked ahead to other dancers to see what they were doing. *Oh yeah,* she thought. She held one hand on the barre and bent her knees until she was squatting close to the ground. She tried hard to keep the weight on both her feet so she wouldn't topple over.

"Everyone freeze," said Mrs. Blair.

"I want you to look at Winifred."

Suddenly the whole class turned and looked at Winnie. She could feel heat rising from her toes all the way up to her cheeks. Zoe smiled at her. Cynthia glared.

"Look at Winifred's body. See how she sticks out her bottom. You do not want to

look like Winifred. You want to be straight. Tuck your tummy in. Keep your bottom down. Now, let's try it again."

The class giggled. Winnie didn't look up. She kept her eyes ahead, her body stiff.

You do not want to look like Winifred. Winnie said the words over in her mind. *Tuck your tummy in. Keep your bottom down.* Winnie held her shoulders back like a soldier.

"Pay attention, Winifred," said Mrs. Blair.

Winnie looked up. The class had moved from the barre to the center of the room.

"Now I will teach you the *arabesque.*"

I can't believe I am taking ballet, she thought. *I could be reading a mystery. Who wants to dance anyhow?*

"That's right, Cynthia. That's right,

Vanessa. Keep your leg in the air. That's right, Joshua. That's right, Zoe. Pretend your arms are floating."

Finally the class ended. Mrs. Blair handed everyone a notice to give to his or her parents. In two weeks, parents were invited to visit the class. After the eighth week, parents were invited to a short recital.

Winnie stuffed the notice into her backpack. It didn't matter if it got wrinkled. It didn't matter if it got lost. Not one bit. Because she, Winnie Fletcher, was not taking one more dance class.

Chapter 8

First Vanessa tried to cheer Winnie up on the way home.

"*Have you got a sister?*" asked Vanessa.

"*The beggarman kissed her!*" replied Zoe.

"*Have you got a brother?*" asked Vanessa.

"*He's made of India rubber!*" replied Zoe.

Winnie didn't say a word.

"*Have you got a baby?*"

"*It's made of bread and gravy!*"

Winnie didn't even smile.

Then it was Zoe's turn to try. "What do you want to wear to school tomorrow? Let's

pick something that Mrs. Russell won't guess."

"Like a hair ribbon," suggested Vanessa.

"Or our Fun Camp T-shirts under our sweatshirts," said Zoe.

Finally Winnie spoke. "I'm not going anymore."

"Not going?" asked Zoe.

"What do you mean you're not going?" said Vanessa. "You have to go to school. It's the law."

"I mean I'm not going to ballet lessons anymore." The girls stopped in front of Winnie and Vanessa's house.

"Don't quit, Winnie," said Zoe.

"Yeah, you know what they say, Winnie," Vanessa said. "Quitters never win. Winners never quit."

"I told you I'd give it a try," said Winnie. "But it's as bad as I imagined."

"Mrs. Blair was pretty mean," said Vanessa. "But she's just trying to help us improve. I want to be a good dancer."

"Besides, it really wouldn't be as much fun without you," said Zoe.

"But you told me you would quit, too, if it didn't work out," Winnie said.

"You want *us* to stop dancing?" Vanessa was nearly shouting.

"You told me you would!" said Winnie.

"That's just like you, Winnie Fletcher!" yelled Vanessa. "You always have to be the boss. You always have to get your way!"

"I do not!" shouted Winnie. "Do I, Zoe?"

Zoe thought for a moment. "Well, maybe you do like things to go a certain way," she said finally.

Winnie felt trapped. *I am not selfish!* she thought. *I just want things to be the same as they were.* Winnie could feel the tears welling up in her eyes. Now she felt like a big baby.

"You two can . . . can take ballet," she stammered. "I don't care. It's good to know who my friends are—and who they aren't." Then she turned and ran into the house.

Chapter 9

For the first time since they were five, the girls didn't know how to act with one another. It was as though Winnie had said *I don't want to be in the end-of-the-alphabet club anymore.* And that made Zoe and Vanessa stick closer together.

On Wednesday, Thursday, and Friday, the girls did all the things they usually did. They went to the after-school program at the Y and they went to Girl Scouts, but things were different. When their troop leader said to choose a partner, Zoe and Vanessa immediately chose each other.

They didn't stop to figure out whose turn it was to be with whom. When Winnie started a chant on the way to the Y, the other two girls didn't seem to hear. But when Zoe started the chant *"Have you got a sister?"* Vanessa joined in right away.

On Saturday morning, Winnie waited until nine o'clock to ring Vanessa's doorbell. Waiting until nine was the neighborhood rule. Calling or visiting before then was inconsiderate since it might wake someone up.

"Why, Winnie," said Mrs. Wiley, who came downstairs in her pink bathrobe. "Vanessa's already gone. Didn't you hear her?"

"Where did she go?" asked Winnie.

"To Zoe's to practice dance steps. Didn't she tell you? Hurry and you can catch up." Mrs. Wiley shut the door and yelled up to Marisa, who was standing at the top of the stairs with a juice carton.

No, she didn't tell me, thought Winnie. *And I didn't hear her. She must have tiptoed down the stairs and across the porch.*

Winnie didn't know what to do. Should she go to Zoe's? She wasn't invited. But she *never* was invited. The girls just showed up at each other's houses.

"I'm heading over to Vinnie's for some groceries," her father said as he came out of the house with an armful of cloth bags. He sat down on the porch steps and began putting on his Rollerblades. "Do you want to come?"

"I'm going to Zoe's, okay?" said Winnie.

"Where's the irrepressible Vanessa?"

"She has to do chores first."

"Oh yeah? Well, be back for lunch." Mr. Fletcher waved and skated up Clementine Street.

Winnie walked slowly to Zoe's. Why had she lied to her father? What should she say when she got to Zoe's?

Winnie could hear Vanessa and Zoe

giggling in Zoe's garden shed. She started heading out back when Zoe's older brother, Karl, called to her. He was raking leaves away from the side of the house.

"Hey, Wee-Willy-Winnie. How's it going?"

"Have any new chants, Karl?"

"Not that I can teach *you*," he said.

Why not? Winnie wondered. Was it because she was younger and shouldn't learn some of the rhymes he knew? Or was it because Vanessa and Zoe didn't want her to know the chants anymore?

When Winnie got to the shed, there was no longer a sound coming from inside. She stood at the door waiting for one of the girls to laugh or say something. There was nothing. Nothing but silence. She looked in one of the windows. At first she didn't see anything, then she looked down. Vanessa and Zoe were crouching quietly on the floor. They were hiding from her.

Winnie ran back home.

All day Sunday, Winnie read mysteries. Sunday night, Mr. Fletcher made Winnie's favorite dinner: orange macaroni and cheese with carrots and orange slices. But tonight the meal looked *too* orange.

"If we had a cat named Mr. Edgar, I'd bet he'd eat this stuff."

Winnie gave a half smile. Dad had read her story.

"Knock, knock?" said Mr. Fletcher.

Winnie didn't feel like playing, but she didn't want her dad to try to cheer her up in a million other ways, either.

"Who's there?"

"Shamp."

"Shamp who?"

"Shampoo your hair tonight, and don't forget the conditioner."

"Okay," said Winnie. "I'll do it now." She put her dish in the dishwasher and went to her room.

What should she wear tomorrow? For the first time, Winnie didn't have a clue how to dress the same as Vanessa and Zoe. Her throat felt tight. Her life was falling apart and no one cared.

Winnie took a shower. Then she went to her desk and wrote a note.

Dear Vanessa,

    I miss you. I want things to be back the way they have always been. I'll take ballet.

    Your friend (I hope), Winnie

Winnie opened her window, put the note in a cup that was hanging by a rope, and rang an old cowbell. Then she waited, hoping.

Yes! The cup began to lift into the air. Vanessa was pulling on it.

The girls had rigged this message system when they'd both had chickenpox. They never talked on the phone when they could use the cup.

Winnie waited. Finally a bell rang from outside Vanessa's window and the cup reappeared. Inside was a note.

Dear Winnie,

I'm sorry I called you bossy. I just didn't want to stop taking ballet. And I think you're

a great dancer, no matter what Mrs. Blair
(Mrs. Glare—ha, ha) says.

What do you want to wear tomorrow?

Love, Vanessa (the fancy dressa—ha, ha)

Winnie wrote back:

How about our friendship anklets?
I'll call Zoe.

Love, Winnie

After talking to Zoe, Winnie knew that
she would sleep well—for one night anyway. Monday night she'd have to start
worrying about ballet class all over again.

Chapter 10

When Tuesday arrived, Winnie tried to act cheerful.

"What's gray and pink and wobbly all over?" she asked while the girls pulled on their tights and leotards.

"What?" asked Zoe and Vanessa together.

"An elephant in a tutu!" Winnie said, giggling.

"I know one," said Cynthia. "What's black and pink and waddles?"

"A duck in a tutu?" asked a girl named Sara.

"No," said Cynthia. "Winnie in a tutu!"

Cynthia stuck her bottom in the air and began walking around the changing room.

"That's not funny, Cynthia!" cried Vanessa.

Winnie gave Cynthia her meanest look.

"Girls," called Mrs. Blair, a few minutes later. "Come out here and sit down on the floor. I want to talk to you."

The girls walked out into the gym. Vanessa sat on one side of Winnie; Zoe sat on the other.

"Today we will practice what we've learned so far. I will also teach you another jump. At the end of class, I will choose some of you to demonstrate dance movements for the parents next week. Now, let's get to work at the barre."

I can do this, thought Winnie. *I will show Mrs. Blair.* She found her place at the barre and held on with one hand.

First they did *pliés. Keep my tummy in. Keep my bottom down. Keep my back straight,* thought Winnie.

Next, they did *tendus* and *glissades.* Winnie followed the girl in front of her. *Fifth position, point the foot front. Fifth position, now to the side!*

"*Frappé! Frappé!*" Mrs. Blair called out.

Winnie remembered that *frappé* meant

to kick her leg so the ball of her foot brushed the floor. *Kick, kick. Keep my tummy tucked in. Keep my bottom and my back straight. Don't bend the foot. Don't kick too high.* There was so much to remember!

"Good, class. Good!"

Winnie smiled. She looked over at Mrs. Blair as if to say, *Look I'm doing it!* But when she did, she lost her concentration.

"Not too high, Winnie. Point your foot," said Mrs. Blair.

Winnie sighed.

The work in the center of the floor did not go much better. Either she started to plot ways to get back at Mrs. Blair and lost her place, or she thought too hard about how to move her body and she couldn't keep up.

"Winnie," said Sara. "You keep bumping into me!"

"Move back, Winnie, so you don't bump the other children," said Mrs. Blair.

Winnie moved back.

"Now I will teach you the *grand jeté*," said Mrs. Blair. "This is one of the most exciting jumps in ballet."

Great, thought Winnie. *I can't do the little jumps right. How am I going to do this?*

"Winnie!" whispered Vanessa.

Winnie looked over at her friend. Vanessa nodded toward the door.

"Pay attention, class!" said Mrs. Blair.

Winnie looked at Mrs. Blair. Then she sneaked a peek at the door. *Oh, no!* Mr. Fletcher was standing at the door watching. This wasn't the day parents were supposed to visit. That was next week! What was her father doing here?

Winnie hoped Mrs. Blair wouldn't notice.

She hoped the other kids, especially Cynthia, wouldn't notice.

She hoped she wouldn't mess up too badly on the jumps.

"Point one toe. Lift your arms in the air,

and step, lift, step!" called Mrs. Blair. "Come down softly as a snowflake."

Winnie pointed her toe. She lifted her arms in the air. *Step, lift, step, BOOM!* Winnie landed like the elephant in the tutu. The class turned around. Mrs. Blair just looked at Winnie.

At the end of class, Mrs. Blair announced the girls and boys who would be demonstrating dance steps next week. Zoe was going to demonstrate *tendus.* Vanessa and Henry were going to demonstrate *frappés.* Cynthia was going to demonstrate the *grand jeté.* "It's obvious that you've had prior instruction, Cynthia," said Mrs. Blair.

Winnie and another girl would pass out the invitations to the recital.

Winnie looked over at her father. He looked different to Winnie. He looked hurt.

Chapter 11

"Start home without me," Winnie told Zoe and Vanessa. She walked over to her father. The others ran to the changing rooms to get dressed. Mrs. Blair gave a little wave to Mr. Fletcher and then she disappeared, too.

"Well, now you know, too," said Winnie.

"Know what, Win?" asked Mr. Fletcher.

"That I stink at ballet, that's what," said Winnie.

"You remind me of myself when I took dancing lessons," said Mr. Fletcher.

"*You* took dancing lessons?"

"Well, not ballet. I took Mrs. Devine's

ballroom dance classes. We had to bow as we asked the girls to dance with us. I had two left feet and I would sweat a lot, so none of the girls wanted me to ask them."

"Why did you take dance lessons?" asked Winnie.

"Grandma made me. I would have been much happier juggling or playing Capture the Flag, but I didn't have a choice."

"It sounds awful," said Winnie.

"Yeah, but I improved."

"How?"

"Come here. I'll show you," said Mr. Fletcher as he walked to the middle of the gym floor.

Winnie didn't want to follow her father. She was afraid that Mrs. Blair or Cynthia or someone would come back. She was worried that her father was going to try and teach her a ballroom step and she had had enough embarrassment for one day. She wished that she and her father could just go home and forget all about dancing.

"I used the Fletcher imagination," said her dad. "I started to pretend that the girls were bumper cars and I steered them around the room. And if I was going to do the—what did she call it?"

"The *grand jeté*." said Winnie.

"The *grand jeté*—I would imagine I was a plane soaring into the air . . ." Mr. Fletcher pointed one toe, lifted his arms in the air, and jumped. Step, lift, step, BOOM! "Only, next time I'd pretend I had to land without a sound."

Step, lift, step. Step, lift, step. Mr. Fletcher

began to do *grand jetés* all around the gym. Winnie laughed.

"Now you use the Fletcher imagination," he said.

"Okay," said Winnie. "I'm a penguin. And everyone knows penguins can't fly."

"But what if you could?" asked Mr. Fletcher. "What if you were the first penguin who got wings that worked?"

Winnie could tell that her father was serious. He really wanted her to pretend she was a penguin that could fly. She wondered if this was the way he sounded when he was teaching college kids.

This is so weird. She pointed one toe and raised her arms. Step, lift, step, BOOM! She slipped and fell on her bottom.

"That's exactly what you did the first

time you tried to walk," said Mr. Fletcher.
"Try it again."

I can't believe this. Winnie thought about being a penguin. Then she tried again. Step, lift, step. Step, lift, step. She imagined herself flying. Step, lift, step. Step, lift, step. "I'm doing it! I'm doing it!" Winnie yelled.

"Ork, ork!" said Mr. Fletcher. He flapped his arms. He leaped in the air. The two of them did *grand jetés* all around the gym.

Winnie didn't care if someone saw them now or not.

"Did my mother dance?" asked Winnie on the walk home.

"Not a bit. She thought she was clumsy," said Mr.

Fletcher. "But she had a great imagination. And she loved to laugh. She would have loved being a penguin with you."

Chapter 12

"Did you see all the parents here?" asked Zoe nervously as she put on her black skirt in the changing room.

"Yeah," said Vanessa. "I'll probably fall on my face."

"Well that's one good thing about passing out the invitations," said Winnie. "I'm not nervous at all!" Which wasn't exactly true. She wondered if her father would say something to Mrs. Blair about Winnie not demonstrating any of the dance steps.

Mrs. Blair called everyone out to the dance floor.

Mr. Fletcher was sitting in the front row. Winnie held up the invitations and gave him a little smile.

"Good luck, you guys," she said.

Zoe and Vanessa didn't need luck. They had prac-ticed their steps all week. Zoe was straight as a flagpole when she did her *tendus,* and Vanessa did *frappés* as if she were a famous ballerina who had been working at the barre all her life.

"And now," said Mrs. Blair. "Cynthia

will demonstrate the *grand jeté*."

Mrs. Blair put on some music and signaled for Cynthia to jump. But Cynthia didn't move. She looked frightened. Too frightened to dance. Mrs. Blair went over to Cynthia and put her arm around her. She whispered in her ear. Cynthia remained frozen.

Mrs. Blair looked flustered. "Would anyone else like to show the parents the jump we learned last week?

"Carol? Henry?" Both Carol and Henry shook their heads—*no.*

Winnie raised her hand. Zoe looked at her with surprise in her eyes. Mrs. Blair didn't seem to see Winnie.

"Zoe? Marguerite?" Zoe shook her head.

Marguerite shook her head. Winnie kept her hand up.

Mrs. Blair looked over at Mr. Fletcher. "Well, Winifred," she said, "it's good of you to offer, especially since we just learned this jump *last* week."

Mrs. Blair started the music again. Winnie closed her eyes for a moment and pretended she was a penguin who had just

been given a special pair of wings. She would show all the other birds, even the nonbelievers, that she could fly, too. She took a deep breath, pointed one toe, raised her arms, and did step, lift, step. Step, lift, step. Step, lift, step. With each *grand jeté*, she landed gracefully. Well, fairly gracefully.

Everyone clapped, especially Zoe and Vanessa. Especially Mr. Fletcher. Even Mrs. Blair clapped. Cynthia glared.

"Why, Winifred!" Mrs. Blair said. "That was wonderful! But remember to stay up on your toes. Parents, I want to remind you of our special performance on the last week of class. Winifred will lead the other boys and girls in leaping across the stage."

"Winnie!" exclaimed Vanessa as she hugged her.

"When did you learn the jump?" asked Zoe.

"My dad helped me after class last week," Winnie said proudly.

"Your *dad?*" asked Vanessa.

"Your dad?" asked Zoe. "Wow! Now you're going to lead the jumps in the performance."

Winnie pictured herself in the sparkly tutu that Mrs. Blair had shown them weeks ago. She pictured herself doing *frappés* and *tendus* and *grand jetés* across a lighted stage. She got that same tight feeling in her throat.

"I know this is going to sound strange," said Winnie. "But I'm not going to take ballet lessons anymore."

Before Vanessa or Zoe could say anything, Winnie continued. "You both love dancing. I want to do things that I love to do, too."

"But—" Vanessa began.

Winnie held her hand up. "I don't want you guys to quit taking lessons."

"But we've always been together," said Zoe. "It won't be the same."

"Yeah. What will you do when we're at lessons? What will you do when we're practicing day and night for the performance?" asked Vanessa.

"I don't know," said Winnie. "I want everything to stay the same, too. But I don't think it can."

"You are so stubborn, Winnie Fletcher!" said Vanessa, but she didn't look as mad as she sounded.

Winnie didn't answer. She went over to tell Mrs. Blair that she wouldn't be leading the jumps after all.

Chapter 13

The next day, smack in the middle of math class, Winnie came up with a plan. A plan for a way to do what she loved to do, and to be with her friends.

"Mr. Barth, can I stay in for recess?"

"You can't stay in here, I have a meeting. But you can stay in Mrs. Twitchell's classroom."

Mrs. Twitchy's name is really Mrs. Twitchell? thought Winnie.

She didn't want to go to Mrs. Twitchell's room again, but she did want to work on her plan. She hoped Mr. Barth would tell the teacher that she didn't *have* to stay in for recess, she *chose* to.

Mr. Barth spoke with Mrs. Twitchell for a moment and then left. Mrs. Twitchell curled her finger at Winnie the way Winnie's grandmother did when she wanted Winnie to come closer.

Winnie got up and went up to the teacher's desk. Mrs. Twitchell motioned for Winnie to come to the side of the desk where they could talk privately.

"Did you complete your homework the last time you were here?" she asked.

"Yes," said Winnie. "I had—"

"I shouldn't have ruined your paper," Mrs. Twitchell said. "I get so used to children *not* using their time wisely that I have trouble recognizing when they are. I apologize."

"That's okay," said Winnie. She said it softly. She wasn't sure she should tell a teacher that it was okay.

Mrs. Twitchell just smiled, so Winnie returned to her seat.

She pulled out a clean sheet of paper and started planning her project. She realized that Vanessa and Zoe would have no idea why she was staying inside. She wondered if they would be mad. She hoped that they would be pleased. She began with a list:

1. Sand the floor to get the rough spots out.
2. Sweep the floor.
3. Hang lights.
4. Set up chairs.
5. Hook up tape recorder.
6. Write invitations.

Winnie needed her father's help. But, Mr. Fletcher had been so proud of her, Winnie hadn't told him that she didn't want to take ballet anymore. Finally, that night, she did.

"Are you disappointed?" she asked.

"With you? Never," he said.

"But you were disappointed when I couldn't do the *grand jeté*."

"I wasn't disappointed, Win," said Mr. Fletcher. "I felt bad for you."

"You said I could do anything I want to do, but—"

Mr. Fletcher interrupted. "I said you could do anything you *want* to do. I meant the *want* part, Winnie."

Winnie told her father about her plan. "Will you help me?"

"Would I miss something as fun as sanding floors?" he asked.

So together Winnie and her father prepared the front porch of their house for ballet practice—a place where Vanessa and Zoe could come and practice their steps and where their parents or little Marisa could come and watch. Winnie would play music and cheer them on. *Maybe,* thought Winnie, *I could write a ballet and Vanessa and Zoe could dance it. Maybe it could be a scary ballet.* Winnie imagined Vanessa and Zoe dancing to haunting music.

On Saturday, when the floor of the porch was ready and Mr. Fletcher had hooked up some spotlights, Winnie left invitations for Vanessa and Zoe in their mailboxes asking them to come over at four o'clock.

At four, the floor was ready, the chairs were set up, and the lights were on, but no one came.

Mr. Fletcher came out and sat in one of the chairs that faced the porch at the foot of the steps.

Winnie sat on the steps. "I can't believe they're being this mean, Dad."

"Maybe they're not home, Win. I haven't heard Vanessa's footsteps all day."

"She's probably at Zoe's."

"Life doesn't always play fair, Win," he said. "But maybe *that* explains something." He pointed to an envelope resting on the steps at Winnie's feet. She had been so busy getting ready that she hadn't noticed it. Winnie tore open the envelope and read:

Please come to Zoe's garden shed at 3:45.
We have a surprise for you.

Winnie tore off down the street. When she arrived at the shed, the door flew open. "Surprise!" Vanessa and Zoe shouted.

"We thought you weren't coming!"

Inside the shed were pillows and Zoe's beanbag chair. All around the walls of the shed were used books. Above the books was a banner that read THE VWZ READERS' CLUB.

"We can come here instead of the library to read together," said Zoe.

"Here, we checked this out for you," said Vanessa. It was number 26 of the mystery series.

When Winnie told her friends all about her surprise for *them*, they laughed like old times and agreed on two things: a time to dance and a time to read. Zoe's mother brought them hotdogs and chips, with brownies for dessert. No one mentioned junk food.

"What are we going to wear tomorrow?" asked Vanessa.

"How about jeans?" said Zoe.

"Jeans would be good," said Winnie, "and tiny braids in our hair!"

"With a red bead at the end," said Vanessa.

"I'll wear a yellow bead," said Winnie.

Vanessa and Winnie looked at Zoe. "And I'll wear blue," she said. "On a tiny braid that no one else—"

"Can see!" said all three girls at the same time. "One, two, three—jinx!"

Zoe walked Winnie and Vanessa home.

The girls said the porch looked just like a real stage. They helped Winnie pick up the chairs. Then they said goodnight. They sang,

"Run along home
And jump into bed
Say your prayers
And cover your head

The very same thing
I say unto you
You dream of me
And I'll dream of you.
(I'll have nightmares!)"

Winnie waited until Zoe was down the street and until she heard Vanessa upstairs, telling her mother about the dancing porch and the VWZ readers' club.

Then, keeping her feet flat as flippers, Winnie did a *grand jeté* across her porch floor. *Ork! Ork!*